Secrets
from the
Dollhouse

BY ANN TURNER • PICTURES BY RAÚL COLÓN

HARPERCOLLINSPUBLISHERS

Secrets from the Dollhouse
Text copyright © 2000 by Ann Turner
Illustrations copyright © 2000 by Raúl Colón
Printed in the U.S.A. All rights reserved.
http://www.harperchildrens.com

Library of Congress Cataloging-in-Publication Data
Turner, Ann Warren.
  Secrets from the dollhouse / by Ann Turner ; pictures by Raúl Colón.
    p.   cm.
  Summary: A series of poems describes the lives of a family of dolls and their
servants living in a dollhouse in a young girl's room, from the perspective of Emma,
the oldest of the doll children.
  ISBN 0-06-024564-6. — ISBN 0-06-024567-0 (lib. bdg.)
  1. Dollhouses—Juvenile poetry.   2. Dolls—Juvenile poetry.   3. Children's
poetry, American.   [1. Dolls—Poetry.   2. American poetry.]   I. Colón, Raúl, ill.
II. Title.
PS3570.U665P64   2000   98-6686
811'.54—dc21   CIP
                                                                        AC

Typography by Matt Adamec 1 2 3 4 5 6 7 8 9 10 ❖ First Edition

Emma Speaks

It's a lovely dollhouse, with three rooms upstairs and three down. Cook lives in the kitchen and is often grouchy. Drinda, my sister, is small and blond and proper. I, Emma, am bigger with black curls, and am never proper. I always want to shout when I should not, and wish my legs could run. We can move a little, but the Laws of Wood say we cannot move when either Girl or Boy is around.

Then there's Buster, the dog, and Butler, who holds the door open, and Papa, Mama, and Baby in her white ruffled bonnet. Baby is afraid of the mice. They leave crumbs in the house and wake us up at night. Cat is too lazy to hunt mice. Sometimes Cat comes so close, his breath steams up the window. I do not trust him.

Girl plays with us, but Papa says, "Girl is forgetful. Be careful."

I can look through our door to the window in Girl's room. Mama says there is something called a tree on the other side of the glass. It waves and moves, and I wish I could be in it, like a bird.

I would like to have an adventure, though I'm not quite sure what that is. Papa says it is excitement and not being safe. Just once, I would like to go outside to the place where the tree grows.

Mama

Mama has round red cheeks
and a lemon yellow dress
that swoops with lace.
I like it best when I
am by Mama's side,
and we lean together
like two trees in the yard.
Then I whisper secrets
in her ear.

Papa

Papa is serious.
He wears his face
like a stiff hat
he cannot take off.
But once when Girl
put Baby in his arms,
I saw him smile
and wink his eye.

Cook

Cook is in an uproar.
All the flounces on her dress
stick out like angry tongues.
She holds her spoon and shouts
she cannot cook
with no meat,
no sugar, and no milk.
But Girl left a pinch of flour,
a dusting of sugar,
and a cup of milk on the counter.
Now Cook smiles
and promises a pudding
for supper.

Butler

I asked Butler,
"Have you ever had an adventure?"
He answered, "Once
I went for a ride on Boy's bicycle.
The world hurt my ears,
and the road made me dizzy."
I decided to lie by the door
next time
so Boy would take *me* out
instead.

Outside

Girl took me outside today!
Something fierce and cold
blew my hair and clothes.
Tiny white handkerchiefs
fell from the sky.
When Girl talked,
her words were clouds.
I was so excited I squeaked,
but She did not hear.
I sat in a tree
and watched a red bird.
What things I will have
to tell Mama!

Soldiers

Butler is gone,
Papa too,
with rifles in their hands
and tall red hats,
soldiers for Boy's war game.
Only Drinda, I, and Mama
are left, holding empty cups
of acorn tea
and wondering what
War is.

Bold Mice

The mice are back again!
They are bold
and scamper in our kitchen,
putting twitchy paws
on lids and pans.
One even bit Baby's hat,
and Baby screamed.
I rocked and tilted until
I fell on that mouse
and frightened him away!

War

There was no warning as
Boy's sweaty hands wrapped
us in bright uniforms and hats.
He put us in the tall grass
where thunder boomed,
something roared, and Boy
crashed Mama and Papa together.
Girl grabbed us,
tore off the hats and cloths,
and put us to bed.
"Poor things," she murmured.
Mama trembled beside me,
and I whispered,
"Now I know what War is:
The hats hide your eyes,
it is noisy,
and you fall down too much."

Cat Comes

We heard his footsteps
padding on the floor,
then Cat poked his paw
through the dollhouse door.
When he breathed,
it felt like fire on my hand.
His eyes shone like green lamps,
but Drinda jerked forward,
fell against his whiskers,
and Cat ran away!

Pictures

Girl took me outside today
and put me by a purple leaf.
A snake stared with eyes of glitter,
and Girl ran away.
When I awoke,
darkness was floating down
on the garden,
catching on petals,
covering my face like a cold blanket.
Then lights turned on in the sky
like lamps in a faraway ceiling,
and I saw they were pictures:
someone dancing, a fish leaping,
and a road like white dust shining.
When Girl came, I was sad to go inside
where there are no pictures
on the ceiling.

Prepare

Papa says we must
arm ourselves against Cat.
"Not to be trusted!" he says.
Buster and Butler will guard
the door, Cook has her spoon,
and Papa knocked four splinters
from the wall for spears.
But I am afraid;
how can we fight
a cat with clawed feet
and teeth like knives?

Stolen

Something took Baby!
When Mama heard no rattle,
we looked
and Baby's cradle was empty.
Drinda thought it was the mice,
the covers were so mussed
with crumbs,
but I think Cat took her
and will chew her for breakfast.
How I wish I could run like Girl
and find my sister!

Hope

I was brave last night.

Stiffly I jerked out the door, calling,

"Baby? Can you hear me?"

Far away I heard her cry.

Somehow I pulled myself inside again

and told Mama and Papa.

Mama said, "Don't give up hope."

But who will rescue Baby?

Saved

I will never say a bad word
about cats again.
Cat came last night,
and dropped a package
by our door.
We thought it was a dead mouse.
But it was Baby,
her hat gone,
tears rolling down her cheeks.
A happiness so fierce and deep
made my stiff arms pick her up,
where she settled and sniffed
against my shoulder,
and Papa and Mama cried
tears of welcome.

Together

Girl put us together last night:
Papa, Mama, Drinda, Baby, and me,
all bunched up on two beds
under one spread.
Papa hummed, Mama sang,
while Drinda and I
patted Baby.
I think I want no more adventures,
except I would like
to see pictures in the sky
once again.

Christmas

Wreaths hang upon the door
like hard green candies.
Tiny candles light our windows,
the tree sparkles in a corner.
We sit at the table
with food piled high:
bright red lobster,
plum puddings,
and mounded potatoes.
Baby shakes her rattle,
Papa and Mama smile,
and Drinda and I sit close,
hands touching on the tablecloth.
I silently wish Cat
a happy Christmas.